The Shepherd Boy

ATHENEUM   1994   NEW YORK

Maxwell Macmillan Canada
Toronto
Maxwell Macmillan International
New York   Oxford   Singapore   Sydney

by **Kristine L. Franklin**   illustrated by **Jill Kastner**

The Shepherd Boy

The author wishes to thank Tom Elkins for
his help with Navajo words.

Text copyright © 1994 by Kristine L. Franklin
Illustrations copyright © 1994 by Jill Kastner

Atheneum
Macmillan Publishing Company
866 Third Avenue
New York, NY 10022

Maxwell Macmillan Canada, Inc.
1200 Eglinton Avenue East
Suite 200
Don Mills, Ontario M3C 3N1

Macmillan Publishing Company is part of the Maxwell
Communication Group of Companies.

First edition
Printed in the United States of America
10 9 8 7 6 5 4 3 2 1
The text of this book is set in Baskerville.
The illustrations are rendered in oil paints.

Library of Congress Cataloging-in-Publication Data

Franklin, Kristine L.
The shepherd boy / by Kristine L. Franklin; illustrated by Jill
Kastner. — 1st ed.
p.   cm.
Summary: As a young Navajo boy brings his family's sheep home one
evening, he discovers one is missing and sets out to rescue it
before nightfall.
ISBN 0–689–31809–X
[1. Navajo Indians—Fiction. 2. Indians of North America—
Southwest, New—Fiction. 3. Shepherds—Fiction.] I. Kastner,
Jill, ill. II. Title.
PZ7.F859226Sh   1994
[E]—dc20   92–33441

To my brother, Ben, a shepherd
K.L.F.

For Tim
J.K.

In the Great Southwest
lives a boy named Ben
who cares for his father's sheep.

Each day
in the summer,
when school is out,
when the rains
bless the ground,
when Father
digs in the garden
and Mother
weaves in the shade,
Ben leads the sheep
to a place
where green grass grows.

White-Eye and No-Tail
help Ben keep the sheep
from straying.
When the sun comes up
they go together
over the rocks,
up the wash,
a boy, two dogs,
and fifty sheep.

Across the mesa,
through a canyon,

they travel to
a secret spring:
the place
where green grass grows.

Each day
as the sun slides
down the empty sky,
Ben returns
to his home,
to his hogan,
a good place to be
when Coyote barks
and the night birds scream.

Ben counts the sheep
in the old way,
the way
his father taught him.
One, two, three.
T'áálá'í, naaki, taa'.
Four, five.
Dįį', ashdla'.
But one day,
all fifty sheep
do not come home.
One ewe lamb is lost.
Forty-nine sheep
are safe for the night,
safe from Coyote.

One ewe lamb
is out alone,
alone to face
the Cunning One.
Down, down
slips the sun.
Now Ben and his helpers
must run
to the place
where green grass grows.

Over the rocks
they scramble.
Up the wash
they fly.

Across the mesa
they run
with hearts
that beat like drums
until at last
they come
to the canyon
where the Old Ones lived
and painted pictures
on smooth stone walls.

Beneath the houses
crumbling with time,
beside the spring,
between two rocks,
Ben finds the lamb,
small and lost
but not afraid,
for she knows the voice
of the shepherd boy.

Ben holds the lamb;
he carries her gently
away from the houses,
past the paintings,
out of the canyon,
across the mesa,
down the wash,
over the rocks,

home to his hogan:
a good place to be
when Coyote barks
and the night birds scream.